Listen to the Desert
Oye al desierto

by Pat Mora
Illustrated by Francisco X. Mora

SCHOLASTIC INC.
New York Toronto London Auckland Sydney

Text copyright © 1994 by Pat Mora.
Illustrations copyright © 1994 by Francisco X. Mora.
All rights reserved. Published by Scholastic Inc., 555 Broadway,
New York, NY 10012, by arrangement with Clarion Books,
a Houghton Mifflin Company imprint.
Printed in the U.S.A.
ISBN 0-590-67831-0

3 4 5 6 7 8 9 10   14   02 01 00 99 98

Illustrations executed in watercolor.
Text is 22/28 pt. Meridien.

To my son, Bill,
who helped me see the desert anew
— *P. M.*

For my mother,
always ready to tell me a story
— *F. M.*

Listen to the desert, pon, pon, pon.
Listen to the desert, pon, pon, pon.
Oye al desierto, pon, pon, pon.
Oye al desierto, pon, pon, pon.

Listen to the owl hoot, whoo, whoo, whoo.
Listen to the owl hoot, whoo, whoo, whoo.
¡Oye! La lechuza, uuu, uuu, uuu.
¡Oye! La lechuza, uuu, uuu, uuu.

Listen to the toad hop, plop, plop, plop.
Listen to the toad hop, plop, plop, plop.
Oye al sapito, plap, plap, plap.
Oye al sapito, plap, plap, plap.

8

Listen to the snake hiss, tst-tst-tst, tst-tst-tst.
Listen to the snake hiss, tst-tst-tst, tst-tst-tst.
Silba la culebra, ssst, ssst, ssst.
Silba la culebra, ssst, ssst, ssst.

Listen to the dove say coo, coo, coo.
Listen to the dove say coo, coo, coo.
La paloma arrulla, currucú, currucú, currucú.
La paloma arrulla, currucú, currucú, currucú.

Listen to coyote call, ar-ar-aooo, ar-ar-aooo.
Listen to coyote call, ar-ar-aooo, ar-ar-aooo.
El coyote canta, ahúúú, ahúúú, ahúúú.
El coyote canta, ahúúú, ahúúú, ahúúú.

Listen to the fish eat, puh, puh, puh.
Listen to the fish eat, puh, puh, puh.
¡Oye! Pescaditos, plaf, plaf, plaf.
¡Oye! Pescaditos, plaf, plaf, plaf.

Listen to the mice say scrrt, scrrt, scrrt.
Listen to the mice say scrrt, scrrt, scrrt.
¡Oye! Ratoncitos, criic, criic, criic.
¡Oye! Ratoncitos, criic, criic, criic.

Listen to the rain dance, plip, plip, plip.
Listen to the rain dance, plip, plip, plip.
Lluvia baila-baila, plin, plin, plin.
Lluvia baila-baila, plin, plin, plin.

Listen to the wind spin, zoom, zoom, zoom.
Listen to the wind spin, zoom, zoom, zoom.
¡Oye! Zumba el viento, zuum, zuum, zuum.
¡Oye! Zumba el viento, zuum, zuum, zuum.

Listen to the desert, pon, pon, pon.
Listen to the desert, pon, pon, pon.
Oye al desierto, pon, pon, pon.
Oye al desierto, pon, pon, pon.